Lizzie Logan Wears Purple Sunglasses

By Eileen Spinelli

Aladdin Paperbacks

To Alyce and Joe, Rosie and Sid, and Maryrose,
my more-than-summer friends —E. S.

First Aladdin Paperbacks edition January 1998
Text copyright © 1995 by Eileen Spinelli

Aladdin Paperbacks
An imprint of Simon & Schuster Children's Publishing Division
1230 Avenue of the Americas
New York, NY 10020

Also available in a Simon & Schuster Books for Young Readers
hardcover edition.
The text for this book was set in Palatino.
Printed and bound in the United States of America
10 9 8 7 6 5 4 3 2 1

The Library of Congress has cataloged the hardcover edition of this book
as follows:
Spinelli, Eileen. Lizzie Logan wears purple sunglasses / Eileen Spinelli ;
illustrated by Melanie Hope Greenberg. p. cm. Summary: When her
family moves to a new neighborhood, Heather meets ten-year-old Lizzie
Logan, whose brash and bossy ways make Heather wonder if they can
ever be friends.
[1. Friendship—Fiction. 2. Moving, Household—Fiction.] I. Greenberg,
Melanie Hope, ill. II. Title. PZ7.S7566Li 1994 [Fic]—dc20 93-29104
CIP AC
ISBN 0-671-74685-5 (hardcover)

ISBN 0-689-81848-3 (Aladdin pbk.)

Contents

1

Not Exactly a Friend

I met Lizzie Logan in June, the day we moved to our new house on Mole Street.

My father and my uncle Frank were struggling up the front steps with our sofa. Lizzie was blocking the way.

"You moving in here, mister?" she asked.

Dad shifted the weight of the sofa. "Uh-huh."

Uncle Frank frowned. "Watch out, Susie-Q."

Lizzie gave him a sourball glare. "My name isn't Susie-Q." Then she turned back to my father. "Got any kids, mister?"

I was dragging a bag full of teddy bears toward the house. Dad nodded my way. "That's Heather."

Lizzie's eyes lit up. I couldn't tell if the light was friendly or not. She plunked herself right in front of me. "Is your name really Heather?"

"Yes," I said.

"I hate that name."

Was she kidding? "That's a mean thing to say."

"No, it's not. It's honest."

"Well, I like it. I was named for my mother's best friend in high school."

"They should have named you for somebody else." Lizzie poked her head into my bag. "Teddy bears!" she screeched. "How old are you?"

"Eight."

Lizzie made a face. "Eight? Holy crab cakes! You're nothing but a baby. Good-bye!"

She stomped down the steps.

That girl was goofy. I dragged my bag into the house.

Five minutes later Lizzie was at the door

with an apple pie. "My mother sent this over. It's store-bought. My mom's the worst cook in the universe. If it weren't for Sam, I'd never get anything decent to eat. He makes the best pancakes."

"Who's Sam?" I asked, taking the pie.

"My father, Miss Nosy."

"Thanks," I said, as politely as I could. "For the pie, I mean."

Lizzie turned to go, then looked back. "I wouldn't eat that pie without checking for mold. Those pies hang around Mapley's Bakery for weeks."

I carried the pie at arm's length to my mother. She was unpacking dishes in the kitchen. "Better check for mold before you eat it," I told her. My mother gave me a look. "It's what the girl who brought it said."

At the mention of a girl, Mom beamed. "You met a friend already?"

"Not exactly a friend."

Mom opened another box of dishes. "I

know these things take time, but at least you've met someone. What's her name?"

"She didn't tell me."

"Didn't you ask?"

I shook my head. "This girl likes to do most of the talking."

"The next time you see her, ask."

I was pulling my scooter down from the moving truck when Lizzie returned. "I'm supposed to find out your name," I said.

"Oh, yeah? How come? You with the FBI?"

"Forget it." I wheeled my scooter toward the house.

"It's Lizzie Logan and I'm ten years old," she called after me. "And I hope you're not always this grumpy."

I stopped. "*Me* grumpy? You didn't say one nice thing yet."

She came over. "I was just ready to." She grinned. "I'm giving you a chance."

"A chance for what?"

"To be my best friend."

"How come? I thought I was too young for you."

"Stop asking questions," she said. And then she asked me one. "Do you smoke?"

"Of course I don't smoke."

She poked her finger at me. "Smoking rots your lungs."

"I know."

"Gets them all black and mushy."

"I know."

"Then the black mush turns into worms. A big, fat old worm colony crawling around inside your chest."

That I didn't know. "Really?"

"Why would I lie?" Lizzie rocked back and forth on her red hightop sneakers. She grinned. "I smoke."

2

Willie's

The next morning Lizzie knocked at the door. "Wanna go butt hunting?"

"What's that?" I asked.

Before I got an answer my mother called, "Who's there?"

"Lizzie Logan, ma'am," cooed Lizzie, smooth as applesauce.

Mom came to the door. "Nice to meet you, Lizzie. I'm Mrs. Wade. Please thank your mother for the pie. It was delicious."

"No mold," I said.

Mom pinched my earlobe. "Heather! What's gotten into you?"

Lizzie smiled sweetly. "Oh, that's okay, Mrs. Wade. Heather's just not herself. You know, moving and all."

Dad's voice came down the stairs.

"Carol, where's my underwear?"

Mom groaned. "Gotta go. I'm up to my ears in boxes."

As soon as Mom left, Lizzie rattled the big brown grocery bag she was carrying. "Well, do you wanna go butt hunting or not?"

"I said before, what is butt hunting?"

"What do you think? It's looking for cigarette butts. On the curb. In the gutter. At Willie's."

"Who's Willie?"

"There you go with the questions again."

I tried to explain. "How can I go to somebody's if I don't know who the somebody is? I wouldn't be allowed."

Lizzie sighed. "You know me, don't you? Your mother knows me."

"But I don't know Willie."

"Nobody does, goose feet. Willie isn't a person. It's a gas station."

"Oh."

"So, are you coming or not?"

I looked back at our new house. Dad would be painting all day. Mom would be unpacking. I couldn't read because my books were still in boxes. I could sit on the porch and watch traffic. Or ride my scooter. Alone things.

"Okay," I said. "But remember, I don't smoke."

Lizzie rolled her eyes. "Of course you don't. You're not old enough."

We walked up the street, searching curbs and gutters. Lizzie found three butts. I found two. We put them in the brown bag. Then we went to Willie's.

"Go ask for the key," Lizzie said.

"What key?"

She smacked her forehead. "The key to the rest room, jelly brain."

I whispered, "But I don't have to go to the bathroom."

"Who said you did?" she growled. "We're looking for cigarettes. There's always tons in Willie's rest room. Besides, do you think I'm going to stand in the middle of the street and smoke? Do you think I want to get arrested?"

I figured it was a silly question I was about to ask, but I asked it anyway: "Why don't *you* ask for the key?"

Lizzie groaned. "*More* questions!"

"Okay." I sighed. "What do I say?"

"Jumping catfish!" she shrieked. "Don't you know anything? Are you sure you're eight? Are you sure your birth certificate doesn't say five? Or maybe even *two*?"

I stood as tall as I could. "I am so eight. I start third grade in September."

"Well, when I was eight," she sneered, "I sure knew how to ask for the stupid key to Willie's stupid rest room."

"That's because you live around here," I told her. "I never lived near a gas station."

Lizzie shoved the brown bag at me. "Hold this. I'll ask for the key. But this is the last time I'm going to do it for you. You have to learn to do things for yourself."

She stomped off. Why was she acting like she was doing me a big favor? I didn't want the old key. I didn't want any dirty old smelly cigarette butts.

Lizzie returned and opened the door. We went inside. Lizzie slammed the door shut. Then she locked it.

Only a tiny crack of light came through the window. The walls were green and greasy.

"I don't like this place."

Lizzie scowled. "See any cigarettes in the trash?"

I peered into the green metal can. "Nope."

"Phooey." She turned the can upside down and sat on it. "Give me the bag."

Lizzie laid the five cigarette butts on her knee. Then she pulled a pair of red plastic scissors from her shirt pocket.

"What are they for?" I asked.

"For lots of things, Miss Nosy. For one, they cut off the tips of these cigarettes."

"How come?"

"You don't think I'm gonna put them in my mouth after they've been in someone else's, do you?"

"Germs?"

"What a genius." She snipped the tip from a butt.

"Aren't black mushy worms in your lungs germs?"

"Nope. They're disease."

"Don't you care about getting a disease?"

"Sure I care."

"I smoke them, jelly brain, but did I ever say anything about lighting them?" She glared at me. "Huh?"

"No."

She snorted. "No. That's right. You can't get a disease if you don't light them."

She demonstrated. She stuck the snipped butt in her mouth. Then she did a lot of posing and puffing and flicking. Her mouth was smirky, like a sideways teardrop.

I made a mistake: I laughed. "That's not smoking. That's pretending."

She pulled out the cigarette. She held it in front of my face. "If it's just pretending, you smoke one."

I backed away. "Oh, no."

"Why not?" she taunted. "It's only pretend."

"Okay. It's not pretend." I changed the subject. "What else do you use the scissors for?"

Lizzie threw the cigarette on the floor and scrunched it with the heel of her sneaker. "None of your beeswax!"

3

Lizzie Logan Is Dangerous

Later that week I was riding my scooter down Mole Street. A girl in a flouncy pink sundress appeared. "Hi! You must be the new girl. I'm Kayleen Bitterman."

"I'm Heather Wade."

Kayleen grabbed my hand and pulled me after her. She ducked behind a telephone pole and leaned close to my ear. "I want to warn you about Lizzie Logan."

"Lizzie?"

Kayleen nodded. "Don't play with her. No one around here does."

"Why not?"

"She's horrible. Her whole family's messed up."

"What do you mean?"

Kayleen sniffed. "For one thing, she

doesn't have a father."

That was news. "She told me she had a father. He makes great pancakes."

Kayleen laughed. "Oh, *that* guy. That's not her father. That's Sam. He's just her mom's boyfriend."

"Where's her real father?"

"Some people say California. But if you want to know, I think he's in jail."

"Why do you think that?"

Kayleen raised one eyebrow. "If you knew Lizzie, you wouldn't ask."

"Well, if Lizzie's father is in jail, I don't think it's fair to blame her."

"Oh, yeah?" Kayleen wagged her finger at me. "They probably arrested him because Lizzie smokes. Parents are responsible for their kids, you know."

I laughed. "Lizzie doesn't really smoke. It's all pretend."

"Well, hang out with her if you want," said Kayleen. "But remember, I warned you.

Lizzie Logan is dangerous."

Just then a voice called. "Kayleeeeeen, time to go shopping."

Kayleen backed off. "That's my mom. I'm getting new shoes today. Two pairs." She ran up the street.

I scootered back home. Mom was putting books on the living room shelves. I plopped down beside her. "Met another girl," I said.

"Oh? Who?"

"Kayleen Bitterman. She lives up the street."

Mom blew the dust from the dictionary. "Do you like her as much as Lizzie?"

I handed her the next book. "I'm not sure I like either one."

Mom set the book down. She stared at me. "Tell me why."

"Lizzie is too—I don't know—old."

Mom smiled. "She's only ten."

"Yeah, and I'm eight."

"Sara Martin from the old neighborhood is ten. You and Sara are friends."

"Mom, Lizzie Logan isn't *anything* like Sara Martin."

"I see. Well, what about Kayleen."

"Oh, I don't know. She seems kind of mean."

"How's that?"

"She said Lizzie's real dad is in jail. She said it kind of happy-like."

"Poor Lizzie."

"Yeah. It must be awful having a dad in jail."

"Oh, I mean poor Lizzie to have people saying such things." She pulled out Volume I of the encyclopedia. "It might not be true."

"You think so?"

"Not everything you hear about people is true."

"Kayleen also said the man in the house isn't even a relative. He's just Mrs. Logan's boyfriend."

"That," said mom, zeroing in on my eyes, "comes under the category of Mrs. Logan's business."

"So I'm still allowed to play with Lizzie?"

"You haven't told me anything that bothers me. Let's see how things go. Seems to me Lizzie could use a friend."

"Mom, do *you* think their family is a mess?"

Mom laughed. "Sweetie, all families have messes. Besides, Mrs. Logan was very nice to send that pie over."

I handed Mom Volume II of the encyclopedia. "Maybe I'll give Lizzie another chance."

1
Killer Plant

It seems that Mrs. Campbell, the previous owner of our house, was eaten by a spider plant.

Or so Lizzie Logan told me.

"I don't believe you," I said.

"Do best friends lie to each other?" she said.

"Maybe not lie. Maybe joke. Plants don't eat people. Even I know that." I didn't ask how we came to be best friends already.

Lizzie retied her sneaker. "Didn't you ever hear of that humongous man-eating plant in the jungles of South America? Ate a whole tribe once?"

"No."

"That's because you watch all those

baby cartoons, Heather. You gotta start watching public television. You might learn something."

"Mom told me Mrs. Campbell was ninety-three. She died of old age."

Lizzie snorted. "Nobody dies of plain old age. Something has to kill them. Like a disease. Or a speeding bread truck. Or . . . a man-eating plant."

"Well, anyway," I said, "there aren't any spider plants in our house. Just some dandelions I picked in the backyard."

Lizzie leaned forward, squinted at me. "Have you checked?"

"No. But I can see there aren't any."

She stomped her foot. "Hah! You think a killer plant is just going to la-dee-da around the house? Huh? I'm telling you—that plant is in there hiding."

"Where?" I said, feeling silly to ask the question, but not totally silly. "Mom cleaned everything. Even the old coal bin down the basement where she keeps our Christmas decorations."

Lizzie shrugged. "Suit yourself. But for your information"—her voice fell to a whisper—"four of Mrs. Campbell's toenails were found right in *your* bedroom. You have a closet, don't you?"

I stared at her. For some reason I couldn't speak. I nodded.

She nodded back. She grinned smugly and walked off.

I didn't eat supper that night.

Before I went to bed, I hunted up my old Minnie Mouse night-light and plugged it in.

Then I searched the closet. I checked between my clothes and on the top shelf where I kept my puzzles. I checked behind my shoes and in both rain boots.

Nothing.

Then I had my father search the closet.

Finally I went to sleep.

Next morning at Lizzie's Lizzie asked me right off, "See any plants in your closet?"

"No."

"Did you look?"

"Yes."

"*Really* look?"

"Yes. I *looked*. With my flashlight. And my father looked too."

She whispered, "It could still be there."

"It's *not* there!" I screamed. "And stop whispering!"

"Hey, hey," she said, "take it easy." She draped her arm around me. "Ever hear of camouflage?"

"No," I said, not trying to be nice. "Never heard of it."

"Well, camouflage is like when something disguises itself. Come with me," she said, grabbing my hand.

We went up to Lizzie's room. She pointed to her purple beanbag chair. "Sit."

"What are you doing?"

She pulled out a book. "Looking for something. This. It's all about nature." She turned to a page about camouflage and read it out loud. "See? Some reptiles even change colors."

"That's animals," I said.

"Animals . . . plants." She snapped the book shut. "All part of nature. That spider plant in your closet could probably make itself look like rose wallpaper."

That night I made my father check the closet five times. He poked in it with a broomstick. He chanted, "Come out, come out, wherever you are!" He sprayed air freshener in it. He growled like a bear. He shook my clothes until the hangers rattled. And then he told me he had to be up at 7:00 A.M. and he was going to bed. "If that killer plant knows what's good for it," he said in a loud voice, "it will steer clear of me and this house!"

5

Fishing With Meatballs

"Hey, Heather! Want to go fishing?"

It was Lizzie calling through the screen door.

"Come in, Lizzie," said Mom.

"Hello, Mrs. Wade." Lizzie's tone was soft as marshmallow.

"Where do you go fishing around here?" asked Mom.

"The Winklers'. They have a tiny pond in their backyard."

"And who are the Winklers?"

Lizzie picked up one of our books and leafed through it. "House at the end of the block."

"They don't mind you fishing in their backyard?"

Lizzie set the book down, shook her

head. "Nope. I do it all the time. I'm practicing for when Sam takes me deep-sea fishing."

"When's that?" I asked.

"Next year," said Lizzie, "when I'm eleven. He promised."

Mom looked at me. "Want to go fishing?"

I shrugged. "I guess so."

Lizzie grinned. "Get some string and two safety pins. I got the fishing sticks."

Outside Lizzie said, "See any spider plants last night?"

I stamped my foot. "If you're going to talk about spider plants, I'm going home."

Lizzie crossed her heart. "Won't say another word."

"Good."

We went down to the Winklers'. The back gate was locked. "Guess we can't fish today," I said.

Lizzie swung her legs over the fence. "Ever hear of climbing?"

"Won't they get mad?"

"Fish don't get mad, hamster head."

"I wasn't talking about the fish. I was talking about the Winklers."

"They won't mind. Besides, the Winklers aren't even home."

I peered at the kitchen window. No lights. "How do you know?"

"I saw them go out."

"Maybe they're coming right back."

"They went to visit their grandkids in Philadelphia."

"How do you know?"

"I heard them talking. Now, shut up and come on." She yanked my arm.

I climbed over. "Where's the pond?"

Lizzie groaned. "You got your eyes closed or something? It's right here."

I did a triple take. "That's not a pond. It's a puddle."

"It's water, isn't it?"

"Puddle water, not pond water."

Lizzie snapped, "Water's water."

I snapped back, "Well, I never saw a fish in a puddle."

"Did you ever *look* for a fish in a puddle?" she sneered.

I had to say no.

She smirked. "Didn't think so. Besides, this isn't just any old puddle. It's a deep puddle. If I pushed you in, you could drown."

What hogwash. "Oh, never mind," I said, backing away. "Let's just fish."

We tied string to our sticks and hooked safety pins to the ends. Lizzie inspected her fishing rod. She looked pleased. "Okay. Now for the bait."

I looked around. "What kind of bait?"

"Worm bait, dummy."

"Where do we get worms?"

"In Mrs. Winkler's tomato garden. Here's a spoon. Go dig."

"*Me* dig? Why can't *you* dig?" I put my hands behind my back.

Lizzie rolled her eyes. "You are such a baby. I have to do everything." She began digging furiously. In ten seconds she had the biggest, fattest, pinkest worm I had ever seen.

"You sure that's not a snake?" I said.

"Nope." She grinned proudly. "Just one world-class night crawler. Big enough for both of us." She pulled her red plastic scissors from her shirt pocket. "I'll just cut this dude in half—"

I screamed, "Don't!"

She snapped around and hissed. "Will you shut up! You'll scare the fish away."

"Don't cut the worm!" I begged. "Please!"

"Why not?"

"Because if you do, I'll throw up."

Lizzie growled, "We gotta have bait to catch fish."

I pointed to the Winklers' trash can. "Maybe there's something in there."

Lizzie sighed and dropped the worm. She put her scissors away and marched to the can. She rummaged through it, tossing eggshells, macaroni boxes, tin cans, and crumpled junk mail all over the Winklers' backyard. I kept throwing things back in the can.

Suddenly Lizzie yelped. "I got something!"

She held up a meatball. It was old and crusty and not even round anymore. But it was better than a giant cut-in-half worm.

With her bare hands Lizzie broke the meatball into two chunks. We each hooked a chunk onto the pin at the end of our fishing string. Lizzie dropped her line into the puddle. It made more of a *plip* than a *plop*. She sat, knees up, at the water's edge. She looked at me. "Well?"

I checked to see if anyone was looking over the fence. I dropped my line into the puddle.

We fished.

We fished all morning, till past lunchtime. We caught nothing.

"I told you fish don't live in puddles," I said.

Lizzie gave me her sourball look. "There's plenty of fish in this puddle. They just don't like meatballs."

6
Charley

Dad held up a small pink envelope. "Look who got something in the mail?"

"Me?" I asked hopefully.

"Are you Miss Heather Wade?"

I snatched the envelope, tore it open. Inside was an invitation to Kayleen Bitterman's birthday party.

That afternoon Lizzie stopped by to show me her new butterfly net. We sat on the front steps. Lizzie tried to catch flies.

"I've been invited to Kayleen's birthday party," I told her.

"Whoop-dee-doo."

"I guess she didn't invite you."

"Good thing! I'd never go anyway," said Lizzie. "I hate those itty-bitty-baby birthday parties. While you're singing dumb 'Happy

Birthday' to Kayleen Bitterman, I'll be at the SPCA getting a dog."

I had always wanted a dog, but Dad was allergic to dog hair. "Oh, Lizzie!" I cried. "You're so lucky!"

"You can come along," she said. "Help pick it out. Maybe even help name it."

I shrieked, "Really?" Before I knew it, I was hugging her so hard we almost toppled down the steps.

With a grimace she pried her arms away. "Hey, cool it. Just be at my house tomorrow. One sharp."

I groaned. "One o'clock? I'll be at Kayleen's party then."

Lizzie stood up. She shrugged. "Too bad."

"Can't you go before the party?" I begged. "Or after?"

"Nope."

"But I already told Kayleen I was coming."

"Tell her you changed your mind."

"That would be rude."

Lizzie snorted. "Trust me. Kayleen Bitterman knows all about rude. Besides, who says *you* have to be the Miss Manners of Mole Street?"

I stood up. I faced Lizzie. "I have to go to the party."

Lizzie gazed at the sky. She sighed. "Guess I have to get a new best friend."

Kayleen's party theme was pink.

Pink balloons. Pink party hats. Pink cake. Pink ice cream.

She had invited three other girls besides me: Erica Chapko, Wendy Wilson, and Sue-Ann LeBoon. Betsy and Bootsie, the three-year-old Woolery twins, were there, too, but only because Mrs. Bitterman and Mrs. Woolery happened to be in the same cake-decorating class.

But the twins weren't there for long.

During the first five minutes Betsy poked holes in the cake with her finger. Then Bootsie tried to give Kayleen's cat a bath in the pink lemonade punch. Finally Mrs. Woolery scooped up the twins, one in each arm, and left.

It was time for Kayleen to open her presents.

The first was from Erica. It was a plastic case with three tubes of pink lipstick.

"Oooooo," cooed Kayleen.

Next Kayleen opened Wendy's gift: a bottle of Tinker Bell perfume. Pink of course. Kayleen splashed some behind her ears. "Thanks, Wendy."

Sue-Ann's pink polka-dotted bag contained a soft stuffed bunny. Also pink. Kayleen squealed, "It's sooooo adorable."

I hadn't known about Kayleen's favorite color. My gift was wrapped in yellow tissue with green ducks. Kayleen tore the tissue apart. "What is it?"

"It's an ant farm," I told her. "Ants are fun to watch."

"Gross!" screeched Erica.

"Joey Fryola had one of those," said Wendy. "Once the ants escaped and ate through all the cracker boxes in Mrs. Fryola's kitchen."

Kayleen shivered. "Yuck!"

"Who wants to play pin the posy on the pig?" chirped Mrs. Bitterman, handing out pink tissue paper flowers.

After the games we sang "Happy Birthday" to Kayleen.

I noticed the clock. It was past one. "Lizzie's getting a dog today!" I announced.

Kayleen sniffed. "Who cares."

Erica giggled. "Poor dog."

"I'm glad you didn't invite Lizzie to your party," said Sue-Ann.

Mrs. Bitterman began to cut the cake.

"I have to go," I told her.

"But you didn't have your cake and ice cream yet," she said.

"I'm not hungry," I called as I rushed out the door.

I found Lizzie kneeling in her front yard playing tug-of-war with a black cocker spaniel. "Pull, Charley!" she commanded.

I walked up to her. She ignored me.

"He's cute," I said.

She threw the stick they had been playing with. Charley chased after it and brought it back. Lizzie hugged him. "Good dog."

"Kayleen's party wasn't much fun," I said.

Lizzie gave me a poison-ivy scowl. Then she picked up Charley and marched into her house.

7
Best Friend Dudes

June was almost over. I helped finish the unpacking. Mom and Dad and Uncle Frank had decided to go into the antique business. They rented a shop. It was called The Good Old Days. I dusted the shelves.

I also rode my scooter. Watched TV. Read some books. Played a couple of games of Candyland with the Woolery twins. I even visited Joey Fryola's ant farm.

If Lizzie and I saw each other on the street—and we did, every day—we didn't speak.

She was always with Charley.

She had tied a red ribbon around his neck. She threw an old tennis ball for him to fetch. She walked him up and down Mole Street on a leash.

At first it seemed she was just showing off. Strutting. Wanting me to notice she had a new best friend.

But as the days passed, I could tell she really loved Charley. She'd hug him and laugh. She hadn't been much of a laugher with me. I felt kind of sad.

I thought about trying to make up with Lizzie. But every time I went near her, Charley would bark and Lizzie would look at me as though I were Kayleen Bitterman.

Mom suggested I write a note. And so I did. It said:

Dear Lizzie,
I miss you.
Let's be friends again.

I didn't sign my name. I didn't have to. Except for Charley, I was Lizzie's only best friend. Or ex-best friend.

I used my allowance to buy a yellow

Frisbee for Charley. I wrapped it in the yellow tissue with green ducks left over from Kayleen's party.

I put the note and the package on Lizzie's front porch.

The next morning, when I woke up, there was a note on my porch. It said:

> Come over for pancakes.
> L.
> P.S. Charley says, "Woof-woof."
> (That's *thank you* in dog talk.)

By the time I got there, a tower of pancakes was keeping warm in the oven.

Sam, Lizzie's so-called father, had curly brown hair and a beard. He made pancakes every Sunday after church. It was a tradition.

"Eight for you," said Lizzie, "ten for me."

Sam set a jug of real maple syrup on the table. "Lizzie eats one pancake for each year."

"What about when you're fifty?" I giggled.

"Sam will make them smaller then," said Lizzie. "Like quarters."

The first time I heard Lizzie call Sam by his first time, I was shocked. Maybe he wasn't her father, but he was still a grownup. Mom said Lizzie seemed to enjoy shocking me. Maybe if I didn't act so shocked, she'd give up. When Sam left the kitchen, I decided to practice. "George never makes pancakes," I said.

Lizzie's eyebrows went up. "Who's George?"

"*My* father," I said, smearing the first pancake with butter.

Lizzie's jaw dropped. Had *I* shocked *her*? The idea was exciting. I decided to go all out. "Carol's the cook in our house."

"Carol?" Lizzie screeched. "Does your mother know you call her Carol?"

I shrugged.

Lizzie jabbed a piece of pancake with her fork and popped it in her mouth. "Well, if you ask me, it's downright disrespectful."

It was my turn to screech. "You do it all the time!"

Lizzie gaped at me. "I've never called your mother Carol in my whole entire life."

I poked her. "Don't act dumb. You know that's not what I meant."

"Well, if you mean me calling Sam, Sam, that's because—" She stopped, blinked, stared at me. As awkward seconds went by, she seemed to get small and scared. I was sorry I had pushed her. Just then Charley came to the rescue, sniffing his way into the kitchen. He seemed to be saying, "What's that delicious smell?"

Sam followed. "Hungry, Charley, old boy?"

I offered Charley a piece of pancake. Lizzie yelled, "Don't!"

I dropped the pancake on the table. "What's wrong?"

Lizzie rolled her eyes. "If you feed Charley at the table, jelly brain, he'll grow up to have bad manners."

I couldn't believe my ears. Lizzie Logan worried about the manners of her dog!

She softened. "Put the pancake in his dish."

I started to walk over to Charley's dish. He was so anxious to get at the pancake, he tangled himself in my legs. I went sailing into Sam.

Lizzie laughed. "Charley sure loves your cooking, Sam."

Sam tousled Lizzie's hair. "Just like you, old girl."

Lizzie ate all ten of her pancakes. I ate two. Sam said he'd save the others for Mrs. Logan.

Lizzie and I put our plates in the sink. She whispered, "Let's go to Willie's."

"Why?"

"I need a smoke. Besides, I got something for you."

"What?"

"You'll see."

We walked up to Willie's. I asked for the key to the rest room. That's how it's been since that first time.

Lizzie spotted a cigarette butt on the sink. She took out her scissors, snipped the end, and plunked the butt into her mouth.

"I think you should give up smoking," I told her.

"Maybe I will," she replied. "Just not today."

Lizzie flicked a pretend ash to the floor. Then she pulled something from her back pocket and gave it to me.

It was a package. Gift-looking. Soft white paper. Purple bow (squashed from being in her pocket).

"Hey," I said, "it's not my birthday."

"Who says it's a birthday present, goof-ball?"

"What kind of present is it, then?"

"It's a best-friend present."

"Gee, I don't have anything for you. I mean, I didn't know . . . "

"Just open the dumb thing."

I opened it. Inside was the flashiest, most wonderful pair of sunglasses I had ever seen. Dark lenses. Fluorescent purple plastic frames. Fake rubies. "These must have cost a fortune!" I gasped.

She snorted. "Try them on."

I tried them on.

"Look in the mirror."

I looked.

And right behind me was Lizzie wearing an identical pair. We laughed.

"We are a couple of superbad dudes," said Lizzie.

"Dudes are boys," I said.

Lizzie smacked the back of my head.

"Hey, don't you believe in equality? Equal pay? Equal . . . "

"Okay. Okay!" I turned to view the glasses from different angles.

"Superbad dudes it is."

"Best friend dudes," she said.

I smiled back at her in the mirror. "Best friend dudes."

8

Mom and the Spider Plant

It was the Fourth of July.

Dad was up at the crack of dawn. "Carol," he called, "where's the grill? Where's the flag? Where's my barbecue apron?"

Mom appeared on the steps, white nightgown, eyes half shut. She looked like a ghost.

"Six A.M."

Dad grinned at her. "Big day ahead."

Mom staggered downstairs. She slumped into a kitchen chair. Her mouth opened and out crawled a single word: "Coffee."

We had invited the Logans over for hamburgers. And all the trimmings of course: potato salad, pickled eggs, baked beans. Sam said he would make the dessert.

Uncle Frank was coming too. He'd told me he'd be bringing along a surprise.

"Better not be firecrackers," Mom had said.

Dad plugged in the coffeepot. "What are you and Lizzie planning?"

"We were going to have a parade. A big one. All of Mole Street."

"Fun," said Mom. She's a one-word person till she's had her morning coffee.

"Yeah, but Lizzie got the idea too late. Not enough time to set it all up."

Dad pulled his chef's hat out of the kitchen drawer and popped it on his head. "How do I look?"

Mom grinned sleepily. She patted his belly. "Doughboy."

The Logans came at noon. Lizzie was wearing her sunglasses. I pulled mine from my pocket and put them on.

"Great Hollywood shades," said Sam.

Mrs. Logan handed my mother a round wicker basket. "Dessert," she said.

Mom pulled off the lid. "Ah, strawberry pie! Yummy."

Sam took a bow. "Sam makes just about everything in our house, which is a good thing since I'm the world's worst cook," said Mrs. Logan.

Charley barked. "He smells hamburgers," said Lizzie.

"Did you bring Charley's dish?" I asked.

"Yep," said Lizzie. "The Frisbee too."

Lizzie and I took turns tossing the Frisbee to Charley.

Uncle Frank arrived. "Hello, small people," he said to Lizzie and me. He handed me a bag.

Lizzie's eyes brightened. "Firecrackers?"

Cautiously I opened the bag. I pulled out a jar.

"Let me see," said Lizzie, pushing closer. She yelped. "A roach!"

"It's not a roach," I said. "Is it, Uncle Frank?"

"It's a cricket," he said. "Got it at the pet store." He turned to my father. "Not to worry, George. Crickets don't have hair."

Lizzie clapped her hands. "Crickets used to be popular pets in China. The people would catch them in little bamboo traps. I learned that by watching public television."

"Now you have a pet of your own," said Mrs. Logan, smiling.

"Watch that jar doesn't break," said Mom.

Lizzie and I took the cricket to my room.

"It *is* kind of cute," I said.

Lizzie added, "For a cricket. What are you going to name it?"

"I don't know."

Lizzie peered into the jar. "How about Mergatroid?"

I threw one of my teddy bears at her. "Maybe it's a girl."

Lizzie shook her head. "Nope. It's definitely a boy."

"How do you know?" I asked.

"It's singing. Only boy crickets do that."

We watched the cricket hop around in the jar for a while. "I know!" I piped. "I'll call it Hoppy."

Lizzie hurled my teddy bear back. It bounced off my head. "Hoppy? What kind of noodlehead name is that?"

"Look," I told her, "you got to name Charley. I'm going to name my pet Hoppy."

"Well," said Lizzie, wagging the jar at me, "better fix old Hoppy a proper home."

"What's wrong with the jar?"

"It's too small, goofball. A cricket needs space. Grass. Twigs. Water. Food."

"Gee. I never realized a bug needed so much."

"That's because you never watch public television."

"So what do I do?"

"You can have a hamburger," Lizzie said. "I'll be right back."

She ran from my room.

Ten minutes later she returned with a dusty aquarium. "Hoppy's house!" she announced. "Dug it out of my basement."

We hosed it down till it sparkled. Then we lined it with dirt and grass and twigs. Lizzie filled a soda cap with water and set it in one corner.

Mrs. Logan applauded. "Good job, girls!"

"Needs a lid," said Sam. "Crickets are great jumpers."

Uncle Frank set to work making a lid out of an old window screen.

Dad carried Hoppy in his new home up to my room.

"Set it on the floor," I told him.

He set it on the floor.

"Crickets need sunlight," said Lizzie.

"Put it by the window, Dad," I said.

He put it by the window.

Lizzie stood at his elbow. "I hope it doesn't get chilly tonight."

Dad sighed. "You girls figure it out. I've got hamburgers to cook."

I looked at Lizzie. "Where would you put Hoppy's house?"

"Suit yourself," she said. "Just keep it away from your closet."

"Why?"

Lizzie smacked her head. "Don't tell me you forgot?"

"Forgot what?"

"Mrs. Campbell, jelly brain. The spider plant."

That night I dragged my toy chest to the closet and jammed it against the door. I set Hoppy's house on the table beside my bed. The last sound I heard before falling asleep was Hoppy's singing.

The next morning Mom sliced bananas

on my cornflakes. I poked at them with my spoon.

"Not hungry?" she asked.

"Nah."

"Too many hamburgers yesterday?"

I shrugged.

Mom sat across from me. "What's wrong?"

I sighed. "Nightmares."

She took my hand in hers. "What kind of nightmares?"

"Plants," I told her. "Spider plants with bulging eyes and bony arms and big green fangs."

Mom looked at the ceiling, then back at me. "Heather, have you ever *seen* a spider plant?"

I shook my head.

She pulled me to my feet. "Let's go." She marched me to the car. "We're going to clear up this spider plant business once and for all."

We drove to a greenhouse. We went inside. It seemed bright enough, smelled like sun and dirt. Summery.

"We'd like to see a spider plant," said Mom.

A friendly man in a plaid shirt pointed. "Down thataway. Next greenhouse."

I let Mom go first. The next greenhouse was really warm—hot actually—but I was shivering.

"Ah!" Mom went. "Here's one."

I peeped from behind her. The plant was in a big black pot, like a witch's kettle, hanging from a rafter. It did sort of look like a spider, a giant green spider with spindly legs flying into the air and spilling over the sides of the pot.

"Oh, look," Mom cooed. "This is a baby. Isn't it cute?"

I cringed. I half expected her arm to disappear. Or at least a finger. But she was still there, every bit of her.

She was touching a part that grew out of a long, dangling leg. And it did look like the giant in the kettle, only a whole lot smaller— a baby. There were lots of "babies" hanging down.

Mom reached for my hand. "Your turn now."

Later, when I told Lizzie about the spider plant babies, she nodded. "They're something, huh? Did you ever hear of any other plant in the whole entire world that has babies?"

I had to admit, I never did.

"Me neither. And I watch public television."

"So, fine," I said. "So they have babies."

"So? *So?*" Lizzie's eyes sprang open. "So that's why they eat people. How do you think they feed all those babies, huh?"

"But I touched one," I cried. "Right there in the greenhouse. And I touched the mother plant too." I held up my fingers for her to examine. "Nothing happened. See? Not even a nibble."

Lizzie groaned. "Holy crab cakes, Heather! You're hopeless. Do you honestly think that big old mother spider plant is going to eat you up right there? In front of your *own* mother?"

9

Hanging Out

July oozed along, sticky as a fudge Popsicle melting on the curb.

I was spending Friday night at Lizzie's. We had just gone to bed. The moon was no bigger than an apple slice. In the darkness I finally got the nerve to ask Lizzie about her real father.

For a long time there was no answer. Finally she said, "He might be in California or on Mars. He left when I was a baby."

"Do you miss him?"

"How do I know who to miss? When I was little, I used to imagine that my father was a big movie star. With a red sports car and an L-shaped pool in his backyard."

"What do you imagine now?"

Lizzie's voice floated across the shadows.

"I imagine the truth. He's just some guy who doesn't care."

I wanted to comfort her. "Sam cares."

Lizzie turned her pillow to the cool side. "Maybe."

We hugged good night.

After that Lizzie and I spent almost every waking hour together. Playing with Charley and Hoppy. Fishing. Hanging out at Willie's. Eating. Giggling. Talking. Arguing. Wearing our best-friend sunglasses. Even after dark.

People who didn't live on Mole Street, such as the ice cream man and Mrs. Findley at the Bagel Box, asked if Lizzie and I were sisters.

We'd strut real cool-like, peek out over our twin glasses, and tell them, "Even closer than that. We're best friends."

And then Lizzie fell off my scooter.

She said she couldn't bend her right arm. I helped her home. Sam looked at the arm, touched it.

Lizzie yelled.

Mrs. Logan grabbed her car keys. "We'd better take her to the emergency room."

"Does it hurt bad?" asked Sam.

Lizzie moaned, spun around on one foot, and plopped like a sack of potatoes to the ground. Sam carried her to the car. He got into the back seat with Lizzie and Mrs. Logan drove to the hospital.

I waited on my front porch, pacing. Mom tried to get me to come inside. "You don't know how long they'll be," she said.

"I don't want to come in."

"Then sit down. Relax. You'll give yourself a heart attack."

"I can't sit down. I'm too nervous."

Mom wet her thumb and wiped a smudge off my cheek. I hated it when she did that. "I've got an idea," she said cheerily. "Why don't you make Lizzie a card. You can give it to her when she gets back."

That's what I did. I sat on the big wicker

chair and made a card for Lizzie. I drew a spider. She likes spiders. I drew a pickle. She likes pickles. I drew a teddy bear. She hates teddy bears, but I like them.

On the inside of the folded paper, I wrote: GET WELL SOON!

Finally Mrs. Logan's car pulled up. I rushed over and gave Lizzie the card. "You okay?"

She rubbed her arm. "Those dumb doctors don't know anything."

Mrs. Logan smiled. "Lizzie's fine."

"I am not." She pouted. "I'm terrible."

Mrs. Logan and Sam went in. Lizzie and I sat on her front steps. She glowered at me. "You shouldn't have let me use your scooter."

"But you begged me," I reminded her.

"If I begged you to push me into a vat of boiling onion juice, would you?"

"Of course not."

"If I begged you to cut off my thumb

with these scissors"—she patted her shirt pocket—"would you?"

"No."

"Like I said, you shouldn't have let me ride your scooter."

We sat without speaking for a minute. I tried to be patient. After all, Lizzie had just come home from the hospital.

Then she said, "I could take you to small claims court."

I almost toppled over. "Huh?"

"For lending me your scooter. For my broken arm."

"But your mom said you were fine."

"That's because the doctor who checked me was a noodlehead from the North Pole."

I got up. "Well, go ahead then, take me to small claims court. See if I care." I stomped off.

Lizzie howled. "Don't be such a goose. Nobody takes their best friend to small claims court."

I sat back down, relieved. I asked if she wanted to stop by The Good Old Days. Sometimes Uncle Frank let us run the cash register.

She patted my head. "Okay, but first I have to put a sling on this arm."

Soon Lizzie reappeared with her arm tied up in an old striped towel.

We walked to The Good Old Days.

Uncle Frank was glad to see us. "Will you small people watch the store for a minute? I've got to run to the bank."

With her free hand Lizzie patted Uncle Frank's arm. "Leave everything to us."

As soon as Uncle Frank left, Lizzie poked her head out the door. "Not a customer in sight," she said.

"It's been slow all week," I told her.

"Of course it's been slow," she said. "You're not promoting the business."

"What do you mean by promoting?"

"I mean balloons, banners, freebies." We

both looked around. Not a balloon, banner, or freebie in sight. I looked at Lizzie. "So?"

"So, I'm thinking." She strolled around the shop. "I'm trying to remember the public TV show I saw on business." Then she walked up to a red feather boa hanging on a hook. She stopped. She stared at it. "Aha!"

"Aha?"

"Yeah. Aha." Lizzie took the boa from the hook and wrapped it around her neck. The feather-duster ends fell all the way to the floor. "On the program they said if the customer won't come to the shop, take the shop to the customer." And then she sashayed out the door. "Get ready for the mob."

I saw her walk by the door twice. Swirling the boa around with her left hand. She was calling, "Get your antiques here! Get 'em here!"

Then a silence for a while; then a bark and a growl; then Lizzie yelping, "Get out!

Get out!"; louder growling; then a lady's voice yelling, "Fifi, no!"; then Uncle Frank's voice: "Hey! What the—?"

Then the whole show was coming into the shop: a black French poodle with one end of the red boa in its teeth; Uncle Frank grabbing the other end of the boa; Lizzie in the middle, spinning, the boa wrapped around her; and a lady carrying a big white pocketbook calling, "Fifi! Naughty dog!"

Five minutes later the lady and the dog were gone. Uncle Frank was back behind the cash register. The tattered boa was back on the hook with a price-reduced tag. And Lizzie and I were out of the store-promotion business.

10

Pizza and Pancakes

Three days after Lizzie had fallen off my scooter, Sara Martin, my friend from the old neighborhood, called. I invited her to visit for the weekend.

"She's coming!" I said to Lizzie. "Isn't that great?"

Lizzie burped. "Yippo."

"My two best friends in the whole world get a chance to meet!"

"Whoop-de-doo."

"Don't be such a grouch," I said.

"Who's being a grouch? It's just that if you weren't such a knothead, you'd know it's impossible to have two best friends."

I pushed a wisp of Lizzie's hair back. "And if you didn't pretend to be so tough," I told her, "you'd have extra friends of your own."

She took her scissors and began cutting the grass beside the steps. "I don't have time for extra friends. I have to put all my energy into taking care of you."

I let her words sink in: *taking care of you.* Every once in a while Lizzie would say unLizzielike things. "You'll like Sara," I said.

"I hate her already."

"Just give her a chance."

Lizzie put her scissors away. "Just give me a barf bag."

Sara arrived Friday evening. Mom ordered pizza. We invited Lizzie over.

When Sara reached for a third slice, Lizzie said, "Oink."

Sara's eyes grew big as Oreo cookies. "What did you say *oink* for?"

"Because," said Lizzie, "you eat too much."

"What do you mean?"

Lizzie took a bite of her own pizza. "I've

been watching Sara," she said with her mouth full. "She eats too much. That's her third slice."

"But you're on your fourth!" I pointed out.

"Yeah," retorted Lizzie, "but I'm not f-a-t."

Sara's lower lip trembled. "I'm not fat either."

Lizzie sniffed. "But you're going to be. I can tell by your bone structure."

Sara did not speak to or even look at Lizzie for the rest of the night.

On Saturday morning Sara and I were lying on the floor watching cartoons. Hoppy was napping next to us, in a little screened travel cage Uncle Frank had made.

Lizzie knocked at the door. "Sam's making pancakes," she announced. "Blooooooooooberry pancakes."

"On Saturday?" I said. "I thought Sam only made pancakes on Sunday."

Lizzie gave a big grin. "He's doing it as a special personal favor to me. And you're invited."

"Great," I said. "Let me ask Sara if she wants to."

Lizzie grabbed my arm. "She's not invited."

"But—"

"It's simple mathematics. Sam's making eighteen pancakes. Eight for you, ten for me."

"Sara can have some of mine," I told her. "I never finish them anyway."

"We only have two chairs in the kitchen."

"We could eat in the dining room."

Lizzie sighed. "Heather, this isn't Thanksgiving."

I stared Lizzie right in the nose. I said, "Thanks, but not today. I have company."

Lizzie raised her sunglasses. "You mean no?"

"Sorry. Maybe next week."

Lizzie kicked the door and stomped off. "Maybe next century."

On Saturday afternoon Sara and I took turns on my scooter. Lizzie came over, adjusting her striped towel sling. She hissed in my ear, "Bet your scooter doesn't go and break Sweetie-Sara's arm."

After supper Sara and I were blowing bubbles in the backyard.

Lizzie walked by with Charley. A dozen times.

A dozen times I asked her, "Want to blow bubbles with us?"

A dozen times Lizzie snapped, "Blow bubbles outta yer nose!"

Sunday morning after church Mr. Winkler came to our door. His face was red. He was waving a bar of soap, shouting. "I want every window on my car scrubbed!"

Dad asked Mr. Winkler to calm down. "What's this all about?"

Mr. Winkler shook the soap at me and Sara. "Those delinquents soaped my windows."

Sara and I gawked at each other. "We did?"

"How do you know it was them?" Dad asked.

"Follow me," snarled Mr. Winkler.

We trailed him down Mole Street to where his car was parked. "Just take a gander!"

His windows were soaped, all right. With a message: HEATHER WADE WAS HERE. SARA TOO.

Sara and I spent most of Sunday afternoon scrubbing Mr. Winkler's car windows.

Lizzie came bouncing by. "Keeping busy, girls?"

I glared at her. "I won't forget this."

"Hey, don't go blaming me." She held up her right arm. "I can't write a thing with my left hand."

That evening I put my purple sunglasses at the bottom of my sock drawer. For forever, I decided. It was just too hard being best friends with Lizzie Logan.

Later Dad drove Sara back to the old neighborhood.

Sara got out of the car and waved. "Thanks, Heather. I had fun."

"You and Lizzie not speaking again?" Mom asked just before bedtime that night.

I looked up from the book I was reading. "She's the one who soaped Mr. Winkler's car windows," I said. "I don't need that kind of friend."

Mom sat beside me on my bed. She stroked my hair. "Lizzie can be a handful."

"And she tried to make me think a spider plant was going to eat me up."

Mom lifted my chin. She looked me in the eyes. "You don't think that anymore, do you?"

"Nah."

"Good."

"And Lizzie's too bossy. She tries to tell me what to do all the time."

Mom nodded. "That can be annoying."

"Sometimes I don't mind. Like when we go fishing."

"In the Winklers' pond."

I closed my book. "Mom, there is no pond in the Winklers' backyard."

"No?"

"There's a puddle. When Lizzie and I go fishing, we throw our lines in a dumb puddle."

Mom laughed. "Heather, you don't really think there could be fish in a puddle."

"Not really," I said. "But it's kind of fun pretending."

She nodded. Her eyes were remembering. "I know just what you mean."

We sat quietly for a few moments. Then I asked, "Did you ever have a friend like Lizzie?"

Mom smiled. "Yes. Heather. My high school friend. The one you're named after."

My eyes flew open. "*That* Heather. Did she soap windows and tell you scary things about plants?"

Mom shook her head. "No—it's just that we were different. She wore flashy clothes. Earrings long as roller coasters. I wore jeans and sweaters. She liked loud music. I liked classical. She smoked—"

"Smoked!" I squealed. "Lizzie smokes."

Now it was Mom's eyes that popped. "Lizzie smokes?"

"Sort of. I mean, she collects cigarette butts. She puts them in her mouth. It's all pretend. She never lights them."

Mom flopped against the pillow. "Well, I'm glad to hear that."

"I've been trying to get her to quit."

"Good girl."

"Did you get your friend to stop smoking?"

"No. Her boyfriend did. After they were married."

"Do you think Mrs. Logan and Sam will ever get married?"

Mom thought for a moment. She said, "I wouldn't be surprised."

"Maybe Lizzie will be different then."

Mom laughed. "To tell you the truth, sweetie, I think Lizzie will always be Lizzie."

I groaned. "That's what I'm afraid of." I went over to Hoppy's house. I opened the jar of dead flies Lizzie had collected for him. I reached in with my tweezers, pulled one out, and dropped it in the tank. "Well, at least Hoppy will always be Hoppy. He's the same every day. I can always count on him being my friend."

"People are more complicated than crickets," said Mom. "Maybe you have to give Lizzie a little more leeway. She seems to have loads of skills. All she has to do is use them more constructively."

I flopped back onto the bed. "Like how?"

"Oh, I don't know," Mom said. "Writing murder mysteries maybe. Leading instead of bossing. That sort of thing." She kissed the top of my head. "Lizzie's lucky to have you for a friend."

I shrugged. "Sometimes I wonder if she even likes me."

"Of course she likes you. You're sensible. You keep Lizzie from going too far."

I remembered saving that worm from Lizzie's scissors. "Yeah, I guess I do."

"And you're sensitive," Mom went on. "You don't say mean things about her family."

"I *like* her family," I said. "Sam's great. Mrs. Logan is always nice to me. And Lizzie can't help it if her real father left."

"No, she can't. Maybe that has a lot to do with how Lizzie acts sometimes."

"You think so?"

"Could be." Mom hugged me. "You're good for Lizzie. You soften her."

I picked up my book. "I'd rather soften an alligator."

11

Cricket Heaven

On August 14 I brought a slice of apple to Hoppy.

He wasn't moving at all.

I took the screen off the tank. I poked him gently with a pencil.

Nothing.

Dad came up to my room. He lifted Hoppy out of his house with a teaspoon. "Yep," he said. "Looks like Hoppy is gone."

I dumped my gold teddy bear pin out of its white box. Dad slipped Hoppy off the spoon onto the soft cotton. He ruffled my hair. "Sorry, sweetie." He left the room.

I sat on my bed staring at Hoppy.

Losing a cricket is not like losing a

person, or even a dog or cat. I know that.
I understand that. But when the cricket
happens to be *your* cricket, when it has a
name and it's been living in a tank in
your bedroom for over a month, well, it
hurts.

I didn't eat much supper that night.

Uncle Frank called to say he'd get me
another cricket at the pet shop. I told him,
no, thanks, I didn't want another cricket, I
wanted Hoppy.

The next morning Lizzie came by. She
was wearing one of her mother's black
dresses. She also wore her mother's high
heels and black straw hat with a veil over
her eyes and black wool gloves.

"Your uncle Frank told me about
Hoppy," she said. "I came to pay my con-
dolences." She probably heard that phrase
on public television. For a second I felt
proud of her. This was no easy visit for
Lizzie. Then I wondered if it made any

sense to feel proud of someone who was no longer your best friend.

I made my voice sound as grown-up as I could. "Thank you for coming."

"May I see Hoppy?" She sniffled.

I led her up to my bedroom. Lizzie stood in front of my bureau. She peered into the little white box. She tapped Hoppy gently with her finger. "Hoppy was the best cricket in the whole entire world," she said. "When is the funeral?"

I looked at her. "Funeral?"

"Ah," she sighed. "How inconsiderate of me. Of course you're too upset to think about the funeral. Don't worry. I'll take care of everything."

That afternoon I found myself standing by the gate in Lizzie's backyard. She had invited the whole neighborhood to Hoppy's funeral.

"I'm so sorry," she said to me, pulling a long wad of toilet paper from her sleeve.

"Want to blow your nose?"

"No, thanks."

Lizzie blew hers.

Mrs. Logan came over. She hugged me. "Hello, stranger."

Sam poured me a cup of apple juice from the punch bowl on the card table near the house. There was also chocolate cake. "For afterward," Sam whispered.

The Woolery twins arrived with their mother. They were wearing matching pink sunsuits. Lizzie frowned. "Was that the closest thing you had to black?"

"Hoppy got dead," said Betsy.

Bootsie rubbed her eyes. "I liked Hoppy."

Counting my parents, who were chatting with Sam and Mrs. Logan (but not counting Charley, who was digging in the tomato patch), there were nine of us. We waited, but no one else came.

"I guess we can begin," Lizzie

announced. She stepped up to the chair where Hoppy lay in his white box. Lizzie read the poem she had written:

"Hoppy's gone to cricket heaven in the
    sky,
So we're gathered here to say good-bye.
If you must, then shed a salty tear,
For Hoppy's been our friend throughout
    the year."

Lizzie looked at me. "I couldn't think of a word to rhyme with *month*."

Next Lizzie closed the box and handed it to me. "I've decided to quit smoking once and for all. In memory of Hoppy."

Sam and Mrs. Logan said "Amen" to that.

I gave the white box to my father, who put it in his pocket. He was going to bury Hoppy under the sunflowers in our back-yard.

Lizzie sidled up to Sam. "You can cut the cake now."

After the cake was gone and the card table folded, after my parents and the Woolerys went back home, Lizzie and I walked to Willie's.

The veil still hung down over Lizzie's face. I couldn't decide if she looked silly or mysterious.

"You really quitting smoking?" I asked when we were inside the rest room.

"Yep."

"That's good. Better for your health."

"Yeah."

"Thanks for doing Hoppy's funeral," I told her. "I liked the poem you wrote."

She patted my arm. "Sam's going to make a copy for you. That Hoppy was a first-class cricket." She flicked a roach off the wall. "It was me who soaped Mr. Winkler's car windows."

"I know."

"I feel rotten about it. And Mrs. Campbell did die of old age."

"Not a spider plant."

"No." Lizzie lifted the veil over her hat. She took off the black gloves and laid them over the trash can. "I'm not going to ask you to be my best friend anymore."

"Good," I said. "One day we're best friends, the next day we're not."

"Gets confusing, huh?"

"Yeah."

"But if *you* wanted to be best friends," said Lizzie, "I guess I wouldn't stop you."

"No, it's okay."

"I mean, if you insisted."

I nudged the trash can with my toe. "I guess we can be just plain friends."

"Regular?"

"Right."

"Is that what you want?"

"I thought it was what *you* wanted."

She looked away. "It is."

"Okay, then."

She tore off some toilet paper and blew her nose. "We can still watch public television together."

"Yeah."

"And take Charley for walks."

"Sure."

Her eyes sparkled. "Maybe even plan that parade."

"Fourth of July's over," I reminded her.

Lizzie began pacing. "It could be an end-of-summer parade. Flags. Floats . . . "

"Music?"

"Sure! Drums. Horns." The snap and crackle of her voice was back.

"Where?"

"Up and down Mole Street."

"Who'd come?"

"Are you kidding? Everybody'd come. Everybody loves a parade."

I caught Lizzie's excitement. "Yeah! I'll help plan it."

She lifted me off the ground and swung me around. "Let's get outta here. We got stuff to do!"

12

Queen of the Parade

"You're going outside the lines," Lizzie complained.

"My hand is tired." I wiggled my fingers. "I already colored in twenty American flags." We were making posters to advertise the Mole Street Parade. Mrs. Logan had drawn them and Sam had photocopied them at work.

Lizzie shoved another stack of posters at me. "Some people are willing to die for their country. Can't you at least color the flags right?"

I rolled my eyes. "This isn't for the country. It's for Mole Street."

"Same thing," she said.

When the posters were finally done, we tacked one up on every tree and telephone pole.

"Now we have to get sponsors," said Lizzie.

"Sponsors? What are they?"

"People who donate money. You know, so we can buy prizes for the winners in the parade."

"There's going to be winners?"

"Of course!" Lizzie flopped onto the grass. "All parades have winners. Why would anyone march in a parade unless there were prizes and winners? Huh?"

I shrugged. "For the fun of it?"

Lizzie whistled through her teeth. "Holy crab cakes! A parade isn't fun. It's work. It's marching for miles in the hot sun. It's getting so thirsty you can't feel your own spit. It's your feet aching so much you think they were stomped by an elephant."

"So how do we get sponsors?"

"We ask people, that's how. You'll do the asking. I'm too busy."

"With what?"

She smacked her forehead. "With being the grand marshal, that's with what."

"Oh," I said, "so *you're* going to be the grand marshal?"

Lizzie shot up like a firecracker. "That does it. I'm going home."

"Fine," I said. "If I can't ask a simple question—"

Lizzie sat down again. "Okay. The parade was my idea—right?"

I had to agree.

"But if *you* want to be the grand marshal . . . " She went on as though I were a crabby two-year-old.

"No, thanks. I wouldn't even know how to be one. I was never in a parade before." Which was all true.

"Right," said Lizzie. "And I'm nice enough to let you experience your first parade ever."

I made a great bow. "Oh, thank you, grand marshal."

She glared. "Are you going to get sponsors or not?"

I took a deep breath. "All right."

"Good. Start with your dad. Ask if The Good Old Days will sponsor us."

"How much do I ask for?"

She thought for a minute. "Ask for a hundred, but take whatever they give you."

When I asked Dad for a hundred, he laughed. He took out his wallet. "Here's two big ones from The Good Old Days." He handed me two dollar bills.

Uncle Frank added fifty cents.

Lizzie took the money from me and stuffed it into her red hightops.

"Okay—we'll go up and down the block," she said. "You get the sponsors. I'll sign up the marchers."

By three-thirty we had eight dollars in sponsor money. Lizzie's sneakers were bulging.

Four kids had signed up to march.

Only one place was left for us to go. The Bittermans'.

Kayleen was sitting on her front porch, painting her toenails. Her greeting was plain enough. "Get off my property," she said.

"It's your mother's property," said Lizzie. "We came to see her."

Kayleen blew on her big pink toenail. "I can't get her. I'm too busy."

Lizzie snatched Kayleen's nail polish. "I'll show you busy. I'm gonna—"

Mrs. Bitterman came to the door. "Hello, girls."

Lizzie shifted into her applesauce voice. "—buy some of this great nail polish for my mother. You should wear it for the parade, Kayleen."

"Parade?" said Mrs. Bitterman.

Lizzie smiled. "Yep. We came to tell Kayleen she's been elected queen of the Mole Street Parade."

"Queen . . . ?" Mrs. Bitterman began to glow.

"Yep," Lizzie continued. "The queen gets to ride on a fancy float. And she wears a jeweled crown, naturally."

Kayleen snorted. "I wouldn't be caught dead in any stupid parade of yours, Lizzie Logan."

But Lizzie wasn't paying a bit of attention to her. She was staring like a hypnotist at Mrs. Bitterman, cooing things like "queen's court . . . flags . . . music . . . local newspapers . . . "

"Local newspapers!" Mrs. Bitterman stepped out onto the porch. "Why, Kayleen would be honored, I'm sure."

Kayleen's eyes were dark and mean as cannonballs. "And I'd better win one of those big-deal prizes you've been bragging about, Lizzie Logan."

Lizzie poked me in the ribs. "Oh, Mrs. Bitterman, Heather has something to ask you."

"Yes?"

I cleared my throat. "Um, would you like to be a parade sponsor?"

Mrs. Bitterman smiled like a toothpaste commercial. "Why, certainly, girls. Let me get my checkbook."

13

Prizes and Surprises

At 6:00 A.M. on parade day, I heard a knock on the front door. I padded downstairs in my bare feet. I peeked past the curtain. Lizzie grinned back at me.

I opened the door. "Come over for pancakes," she said.

I rubbed my eyes, yawned. "Gotta ask my mom first."

"Hurry."

"What's the rush?"

"We got work to do."

I raced to my parents' bedroom. Mom opened one eye. "Can I go to Lizzie's for pancakes?" I asked.

She opened the other eye. She looked at the clock. "Six? Pancakes?"

"Uh-huh. It's parade day, you know."

She stared at the pillow.

"Well, can I go?"

She mumbled something and pulled the sheet over her head. I took that for a yes.

By six forty-five I had eaten two pancakes and Lizzie had eaten her ten. Then she ordered me home to get dressed in my parade costume.

"But the parade doesn't start till ten."

"Yeah, but we have tons of stuff to do yet. You won't have time to put on your costume later."

"What about your costume? Are you going to dress up now?"

Lizzie rolled her eyes. "Of course not. I am the grand marshal. My costume has to be a surprise."

I went home. I changed into red shorts and a blue shirt with white stripes. I wore white sneakers and a tiny American flag pin that Mom had found in the bottom of her jewelry box.

At eight Lizzie and I knocked at the doors of all the kids who were marching. Just as a reminder.

At eight-thirty Lizzie announced, "Time to build Kayleen's float."

I screeched, "Don't you already have a float for Kayleen?"

She clamped her hands to her hips. "What do I look like, a magician?"

"No, but—"

Lizzie stomped off to the garage. I followed.

"We have this old wagon," she said, blowing away cobwebs.

"It only has three wheels," I pointed out.

"I got this old skateboard too," she said.

"You're going to put the queen of the parade on a skateboard?"

"No—I'm going to put this piece of plywood on top of the skateboard."

"How?"

Lizzie rolled her eyes. "With a hammer and nails, that's how."

By nine-thirty I was sweaty. My red shorts had smudges on the seat. Lizzie's hair was sticking out like hot wires. Her eyes were black with soot. Her thumb was splotched purple with bruises. But Kayleen had her float.

"Who's going to pull it along?" I asked. "Charley?"

"Charley?" Lizzie squawked. "Do you want him to have a hernia?"

"Then who?"

Lizzie put her arm around my shoulders. "Old pal," she said. "My very, very, very, *very* best friend."

"We are not *best* friends, remember, and I am *not*, I repeat *n-o-t* pulling Kayleen Bitterman down Mole Street."

Lizzie snatched her arm away. "Go ahead, then. Spoil the parade. Spoil the day for Mole Street. For the whole entire country."

Well, I couldn't let the country down, could I?

Lizzie, I had to admit, was a great grand marshal. She wore a blue satin body suit with a red pillowcase cape. She had American flags stuck in her red hightops and a baton in each hand. The thing on her head had once been a simple baseball cap. Now it had gold stars and white pom-poms glued all over.

Charley marched beside her wearing a matching pillowcase and a big blue bow.

Joey Fryola wore brown cut-offs and an old white T-shirt. The only thing patriotic about him was the flag he held. He waved it whenever Lizzie bopped her batons his way.

The Woolery twins, in matching polka-dotted sunsuits, made the music. Betsy banged on a coffee can drum and Bootsie tooted a kazoo.

Then came the queen's float. Kayleen had borrowed her cousin's pink chiffon prom dress. Her crown was blue construction paper stapled together and pasted with silver glitter. Standing behind her was the queen's court (in this case, Erica Chapko in her dancing-class tutu).

The horse pulling all this was me.

Lizzie led us all in a couple rounds of "Yankee Doodle Dandy."

And even though Betsy Woolery did throw up, it landed on the sidewalk in front of the Winklers' and not a speck on the drum or any of the marchers.

The queen's float tipped over—but only once.

As parades go, I'd say this one was a success, even if no local newspapers came to cover it.

The problems came *after* the parade.

Lizzie gave out the prizes.

"Hey! These crayons are all broken up," cried Bootsie.

"All the pictures in this coloring book are scribbled in!" Betsy complained.

"What the heck do I want with a shoe-horn?" grumbled Joey Fryola.

Erica Chapko tossed half a rubber snake back at Lizzie.

And Kayleen dropped her prize with a yelp. "This doll doesn't have any head!"

The marchers were all so mad, they left without touching any of Mom's lemonade or Sam's cookies.

"Some big-deal prizes," I said.

Lizzie turned to me. "Don't you believe in recycling?"

"Of course I do."

"Well," said Lizzie, "every one of those prizes was recycled. I'd say that was pretty patriotic."

"The kids didn't think so."

She sniffed. "That's their problem."

"So," I said, "if you didn't buy any new stuff, where's all the sponsor money we collected?"

Lizzie hugged Charley. "I gave it to the SPCA so they can save more dogs."

14
Dudettes

A few days after the parade, Sara Martin called. She wanted me to come spend the night.

I expected Lizzie to throw a fit when I told her.

"That's nice," she said, rubbing a spot of dirt from her sneaker.

I almost fainted. "You're not mad?"

"Why should I be mad?"

"Because you hate Sara," I reminded her.

Lizzie patted my shoulder. "So? I'm not the one staying with her."

Mom and Dad were busy painting the outside trim on The Good Old Days, so Uncle Frank drove me to Sara's.

Sara had fixed lunch all by herself. Peanut butter and jelly sandwiches cut in triangles, canned peaches, chocolate milk.

After lunch we took a walk. It felt funny being back in the old neighborhood. Not sad, just funny.

We went past my old house. It looked the same except for the blue curtains at the window and a new mailbox.

— There were two little boys jumping over a sprinkler in the side yard. Sara waved to them. "Jordan and Jason," she told me.

"I wonder if they have my old bedroom," I said.

Sara shrugged. "I haven't been in the house since you moved."

We turned the corner. The sprinkler had given me an idea. "Want to go fishing?"

Sara looked at me. "Fishing? There aren't any lakes or rivers around here."

"Maybe we can find a big puddle," I suggested. "Or make one."

Sara rolled her eyes. "Whoever heard of fishing in a puddle?"

"It's fun," I told her.

"Well, not to me. Let's play checkers."

That night Sara and I carried the tiny TV from the den to her bedroom. "What shall we watch?" she asked.

I told her about a show on public TV called *The World of Spiders*. Sara shivered. "I hate spiders. They're yucky."

"Maybe if you knew more about spiders," I said, "you'd learn to like them."

Sara flicked on the TV. "Nothing could make me like spiders." She turned the channel to *Cartoon Cartwheel*.

The next day Sara's father drove me home.

Mom was folding laundry in the kitchen. She looked up from a stack of towels. "Hi, sweetie. How'd it go?"

I poured myself a glass of lemonade. "Okay, I guess."

"Must have seemed strange being in the old neighborhood."

"Yeah, it did kind of. I saw our old house."

"How'd it look?" Mom picked a ladybug off one of Dad's socks. "Did they change anything?"

"Just the mailbox and the curtains."

"And what about you and Sara? What did you do?"

"Played checkers. Watched cartoons." I put my glass in the sink. "Did Lizzie call?"

"No."

"Maybe I'll stop by. See if she wants to go fishing or something."

Mom brushed her hair back. "I think Lizzie's mother took her shopping for school clothes this morning. She should be home by now, though."

Lizzie was down on her knees in her backyard. She was wearing an old straw hat and green garden gloves.

"Whatcha doing?" I asked.

"Looking for slugs."

"How come?"

"To take into school," she said. "Fifth grade mascot."

"Oh."

"Want to go to Willie's?"

"Who's Willie?" I asked.

We both burst out laughing.

"You've learned a lot since June," Lizzie said.

This time at Willie's she let me sit on the upside-down trash can.

"Guess what?" she said.

"What?"

"Mom and Sam are getting married."

I jumped up. I hugged her. "Lizzie, that's great! When?"

"Right after Christmas."

"Now Sam will really be your father," I squealed.

Lizzie beamed. "I've already started calling him Dad."

She took her garden gloves off and set

them on my lap. "It's been a fun summer, don't you think?"

"Goofy's more like it."

Lizzie shrugged. "Same thing."

"I hope I like third grade."

"Third grade's a piece of cake," she said. "Trust me."

"Yeah," I sneered. "And spider plants eat old ladies."

Lizzie covered her face. Then she said, "Honest. Third grade is easy. Besides, you'll make a lot of friends. More your age."

I picked up one of Lizzie's gloves. I tried it on. "Yeah, but it won't be the same."

"Same as what?"

"As us."

"Us?"

"Yeah. Us. *Best*-friends us."

"Yeah." She looked at the wall. "I guess it's stupid to think we could ever be best friends again."

"I never said it was stupid," I said.

"You don't think so?"

I shrugged. "Nope."

"I thought we were gonna stick with being just regular friends."

"Well, if you want to be just regular friends," I said, "I won't stop you."

"No—" said Lizzie. "I mean, best friends is okay with me."

"Sure?"

Lizzie grinned. "Positive." Then she pulled out her purple sunglasses. She put them on. "See, I didn't throw mine away."

I pulled my pair out of my skirt pocket and put them on. "Me neither."

We both faced Willie's rest room mirror. Lizzie's hat was tilting to one side. She straightened it. "Well, we're a couple of superbad dudes," she said.

I shook my head. "Boys are dudes. We're dudettes."

"Dudettes?" she screeched. "That's the dumbest thing I ever heard!"

"I don't think it's dumb."

"That's because you have grape jelly for brains."

I swatted her with a garden glove. "When are you going to stop being so obnoxious?"

"When you stop being a hamster head, that's when."

Ah . . . jelly for brains . . . hamster head . . .

We left Willie's rest room. We strolled down Mole Street. In our dark glasses. Best friends. Just like old times.

DEMCO